O9-ABI-250

# CHRISTMAS Is Coming!

*poems by* Charles Ghigna *and* Debra Ghigna

*illustrated by* Mary O'Keefe Young

TALEWINDS

A Charlesbridge Imprint

*For our son, Chip, who makes every day seem like Christmas.*

*A special thanks to Harold Underdown for his inspiration, guidance, and good cheer.*
*—C. G. and D. G.*

*For my brother, Danny, and his family: Marie José, Camille, and Dylan.*
*—M. O'K. Y.*

The poem "Christmas Is Coming!" by Charles Ghigna first appeared in *Humpty Dumpty*, and "Holly Day" by Charles Ghigna first appeared in *Turtle*. "My Box" by Debra Ghigna first appeared in *Ladybug*. The authors wish to thank the editors and publishers of those magazines for their permission to include them in this book.

A **TALEWINDS** Book
Published by Charlesbridge Publishing
85 Main Street, Watertown, MA 02472
(617) 926-0329
www.charlesbridge.com

**Library of Congress Cataloging-in-Publication Data**
Ghigna, Debra.
Christmas is coming!/Debra and Charles Ghigna; illustrated by Mary O'Keefe Young.
p. cm.
Summary: A collection of poems describing a family's Christmas celebration,
from picking out a tree to storing the decorations in the attic for another year.
ISBN 0-88106-113-1 (reinforced for library use)
1. Christmas—Juvenile poetry. 2. Children's poetry, American. [1. Christmas—Poetry.
2. American poetry.] I. Ghigna, Charles. II. Young, Mary O'Keefe. III. Title.
PS3557.H52          C48 2000
811'.54—dc21          99-054194

Printed in the United States of America
(hc) 10 9 8 7 6 5 4 3 2 1

Illustrations done in watercolor on Windsor Newton 140-lb. CP Watercolor Paper
Display type and text type set in Centaur MT
Color separations made by Eastern Rainbow, Derry, New Hampshire
Printed and bound by Worzalla Publishing Company, Stevens Point, Wisconsin
Production supervision by Brian G. Walker
Designed by Diane M. Earley
Printed on recycled paper

## Christmas Is Coming!

I always start humming
When Christmas is coming.
I skip and I hop and I sing.
I always start humming
When Christmas is coming.
I wonder what Christmas will bring.

There's fresh mistletoe
Tied up with a bow
And an angel with soft, shining hair.
There's new-fallen snow
Wherever we go
And a big Christmas tree in the square.

Oh, I almost can't wait
For my favorite date.
I love this time of the year
When everyone's jolly
And there's lots of holly
And Santa Claus soon will be here.

I always start humming
When Christmas is coming.
I wonder what Christmas will bring.
I always start humming
When Christmas is coming.
I skip and I hop and I sing!

## I See Christmas

I see bows and candy canes,
Baby dolls and choo-choo trains,
Tinsel, stars, and mistletoe,
Mittens, sleds, and lots of snow.

I see bells and decorations,
Ornaments from many nations,
Holly, candles, manger scenes,
Red poinsettias, evergreens.

I see homemade pumpkin pie,
Stacks of presents piled high,
Reindeer, elves, and Santa's sleigh—
I see Christmas on the way.

## The Christmas-Tree Train

The Christmas train is taking me
Along with all my family
To find a Merry Christmas tree.
*choo choo choo*

Eleven miles around the bend
The whistle blows, then blows again
Before the tracks come to an end.
*woo woo woo*

Then gentle horses show the way
By pulling us this holiday
In wooden wagons full of hay.
*clop clop clop*

We finally arrive to find
Fresh snow is blowing down each line
Between the rows of spruce and pine.
*whoosh whoosh whoosh*

At last our favorite tree is found,
And so we circle all around
To watch my father cut it down.
*chop chop chop*

We wish this day would never end,
But now we gather with our friends
To ride the train back home again.
*choo choo choo*

## Picking Out a Tree

Christmas trees are such a tease.
Choosing one's a chore;
There's Fraser fir, blue spruce, Scotch pine,
And many, many more.

But by the time we take one home,
All of us agree:
It's not a pine or fancy spruce—
It's now a Christmas tree!

## On Tiptoes

My sister stands on tiptoes
To decorate the tree.
She reaches up her chubby hands
To help my mom and me.

She hangs a golden angel
Beneath a twinkling light,
Then covers it with tinsel
And kisses it good night.

My brother stands on tiptoes
To decorate the tree.
He hangs a little candy cane
For everyone to see.

He fastens underneath a bow
A silver Christmas bell
Beside the tiny wooden horse
Upon a carousel.

My father stands on tiptoes
To decorate the tree.
He wraps a string of colored lights
Around its greenery.

He finds my favorite ornament,
The prettiest by far,
Then lifts me high up in his arms
So I can place the star.

## *Watch Out!*

Everyone is kissing me!
I want the world to know—
No one in my house is safe
Beneath the mistletoe!

## A Visit to Grandma's

Grandma's house is squeaky.
Her wooden floors are creaky.
The faucet in the kitchen sink
Is sometimes very leaky.

Voices echo down the hall.
A clock ticks loudly on the wall.
Yet Grandma doesn't seem to mind
The noises of her house at all.

Branches tap the windowpane
Through winter snow and summer rain,
And gusty winds bend and spin
Her rusty rooster weather vane.

But Grandma never seems to care.
She rocks me in her rocking chair
And says the sounds old houses make
Are like a friend who's always there.

## Grandma's Christmas Cookies

Roll the dough until it's flat.
Press the cookie cutter.
If the sides begin to stick,
Just dip them in some butter.

    Set the oven temperature.
    Grease the cookie sheet.
    Every piece of cookie dough
    Looks good enough to eat.

Shake the chocolate sprinkles on
The cookie choo-choo trains.
Spread the cherry icing on
The cookie candy canes.

    Decorate the stars and bells
    And trim the cookie trees.
    Squirt the beard on Santa Claus
    With frosting made to squeeze.

Dust the cookie angel wings
With sugar just for fun.
Stick them in the oven
And watch until they're done.

    Bake each Christmas cookie
    With extra special care.
    Christmas Day is coming—
    You can smell it in the air!

# Santa's Reindeer

*It's not enough for them to fly and watch a world of clouds go by.*
*Each reindeer has a job to do . . . in bringing toys to me and you.*

Comet follows every star,
Finding houses near and far.

Blitzen holds his head down low,
Looking out for ice and snow.

Vixen checks the wind direction
At each cloudy intersection.

Dasher keeps a watchful eye
On the time that passes by.

Dancer sets a lively pace,
So Santa visits every place.

Prancer taps his gentle hoof
When it's time to leave a roof.

Donder carries lists of toys,
Letters from the girls and boys.

Cupid, with his heart of gold,
Guards their presents from the cold,

*Once a year when reindeer fly, and Santa rides across the sky.*

## A Holly Day

A holly tree,
A holly berry,
A holiday,
And we are merry.

A star above
To wish upon,
A winter's eve,
A snowy dawn.

All red and green
Along the way,
A holly time,
A Christmas day.

## It's Christmas Morning!

The morning sun begins to rise,
I yawn and stretch and rub my eyes
And jump when I first realize—

*It's here!*
*It's Christmas morning!*

While everyone is still asleep,
Down the stairs I start to creep,
Then hold my breath and take a peep.

*It's here!*
*It's Christmas morning!*

I can't believe all that I see
Beneath the shining Christmas tree:
Gifts for everyone—and me!

*It's here!*
*It's Christmas morning!*

## Beneath the Tree

Blue jeans from my mother,
Wool gloves from Uncle Brad,
A sweater from my sister,
A jacket from my dad.

A brand-new winter wardrobe
To fold and put away.
I'm glad that Santa always brings me
*Toys* on Christmas Day.

## Cousins

My cousins just arrived today.
I see them once a year.
Sometimes we go to visit them,
And sometimes they come here.

It happens every holiday.
I think it's so absurd.
At first we stare down at our shoes
And never say a word.

My aunts and uncles always say,
"Just look at how you've grown!"
And then our parents start to talk
And leave us kids alone.

We get out all our favorite toys
So everyone can play.
That's when my cousins come alive
And have a lot to say.

"My doll is cuter than your doll."
"My games are cooler, too!"
"My dad can beat up your old dad,
And I can beat up *you*!"

We tease each other back and forth
Till nothing's left unsaid,
Then finally plop down on the floor
And start to play instead.

We talk and laugh and giggle till
We're rolling all around.
Our parents come upstairs to say,
"You'd better keep it down!"

And when my cousins have to go,
I'm always glad they came.
Although we're very different,
We're cousins just the same.

# My New Skates

I like to race on my brand-new skates
Where the cool winter breeze blows through the trees,
Tickling the back of my neck and my knees.

I like to glide on my skates outside
Where the cold winter wind begins to spin,
Turning me around and around again.

## My Doll

Rachel's doll has ruby lips and rosy apple cheeks.
Laura's doll has fingernails she polishes each week.
Sarah's doll has marble eyes the color of the sea.
My new doll has freckles and a bandage on her knee.

Ashley's doll has golden curls around a china face.
Hannah's doll has petticoats of ruffles trimmed in lace.
My new doll wears overalls for climbing up a tree
And a baseball cap and a ponytail—'cause my doll's just like me!

## Taking Down the Tree

Dad brought down all the boxes;
We've gathered around for the chore.
Christmas was fun, but now we've begun
To take down the wreath from the door.

We unhook the stars and little red cars;
Each branch of the tree is now bare.
The ribbons and lace are put back in place;
Each angel is handled with care.

It's time to round up the trimmings;
It's time to put Christmas away.
It's time to take down the tree that we found—
I sure wish that Christmas could stay.

## My Box

Each day I like to climb inside
My box where I can play and hide,
A cardboard house of make-believe
For teddy bear and me.

I sail my box just like a ship,
An ocean liner on a trip,
Around the world from sea to sea,
My teddy bear and me.

Sometimes my box becomes a train,
A boxcar roaring through the rain.
I shine a flashlight bright to see
For teddy bear and me.

But when my nap time comes again,
My box becomes a bear-cub den,
A quiet place where we can be
Just teddy bear and me.

## In My Attic

It's Christmas in my attic
Each season of the year.
In winter, spring, and summer,
The holidays are here.

Sometimes I climb upstairs to peek—
Just making sure, you see,
That every Christmas ornament
Is waiting for a tree.

I count the painted houses
Of red and white and green
We placed upon our mantle
In a village Christmas scene.

I make sure every candlestick
Is wrapped up good and tight
And waiting for a windowsill
Some cold December night.

I check the wooden Santa Claus
We gently tucked away.
He's sleeping with his reindeer
Inside the wooden sleigh.

It's Christmas in my attic
With ornaments and bows.
Christmas Day will come again—
And I know where it goes.